For Judy, the true woodland fairy.

Text copyright © 2018 by Karen Bell-Brege
Illustrations copyright © 2018 by Darrin Brege

ISBN 978-1-937665-05-0

Printed and bound in the U.S.A.

10 9 8 7 6 5 4 3 2 1

First Edition

9864 E. Grand River Ave
Suite 110, No. 244
Brighton, MI 48116
Instilling the love of reading through humor and fun.

Visit us at www.monstermyths.com

BIGFOOT

and the

Mitten

To Lilliana Believe! (signature)

To Lilliana Enjoy! (signature)

words
Karen Bell-Brege

pictures
Darrin Brege

One day as I was hopping by,

I noticed a footprint from my friend, Big Guy.

My woodland friends asked, "Do you think Bigfoot really exists?"

"Sit down," I said, "I have a story for you, with a fantastic twist..."

I found a mitten and as I was taking it to my nest,

I noticed a huge beast who looked distressed.

He seemed very sad, so I asked, "What's wrong, Big Guy?"

He lifted his huge head and, "Bigfoot" was his reply.

He tells me how he thinks he lost his mitten.
Well, the one I found he surely wouldn't fit in...
I mean really, a mitten for a beast covered in fur?
Nobody makes them that big, that's for sure.

So, I ask where he lost it, but he doesn't know.
I'm up for an adventure, I'll help him. "Let's go!"

"It could be someplace
really sandy," he said to me.
That's when I thought
I should just leave him be.

I mean, there's sand surrounding this whole state,
Michigan's bordered by four of the five lakes that are great;
not to mention thousands of inland ones, too,
plus, creeks, canals, rivers, harbors and rapids, to name a few.

Then he remembers something about a bear.
Sleeping Bear Dunes! I think we're getting somewhere!
We climbed and we climbed to see the beautiful lake,
but it's not there, he thinks he made a mistake.

"Umm..." he said, "a tall skinny house with a really bright light."
It had to be a lighthouse, I hoped he was right.
He said there were two, and they were both red.
It had to be Grand Haven, there was fun ahead!

The lighthouses are on a pier with a boardwalk to the city.
We looked around because Grand Haven is just so pretty!
That didn't shine a light on anything. Ha, ha, ha, get my joke?
He laughed and said, "I like cherries." I thought he had sunstroke.

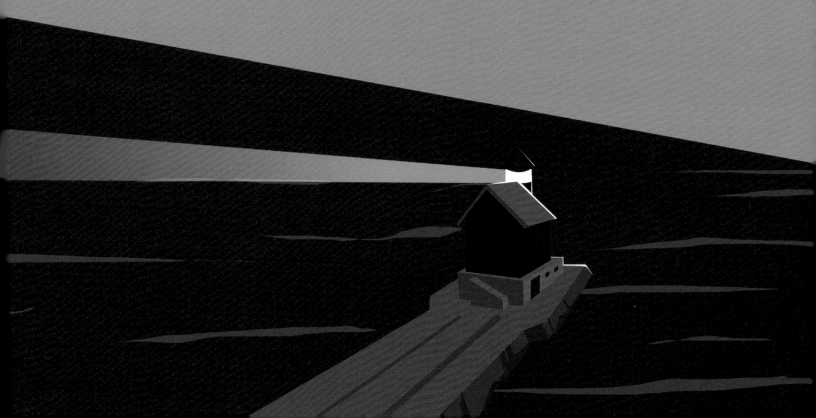

Could it be the Cherry Capital of the world – Traverse City?
He told me finding his mitten there was a good possibility.
I couldn't believe how many cherries he could eat.
If he entered a cherry pie eating contest, he wouldn't be beat.

Traverse City is amazing, with beaches, and a cool town,
art, food, fun, there's so much to do all around.
I said, "Hey, I'm glad we came here aren't you, Big Guy?"
He nodded, said "Bigfoot," and pointed up at the sky.

As he was pointing he tells me, "Up."
I nodded, smiled, and told him, "Yup."
I spend a lot of time up there flying around,
but he continued to point up and not down.

"Up, I get it, Up – U.P. Up!" I told him that
I understand.
He meant the upper peninsula – the top of
Michigan's hand!
It's northern Michigan, from
Tahquamenon Falls and
Pictured Rocks
to Escanaba, Marquette, Isle
Royale, and the Soo Locks.

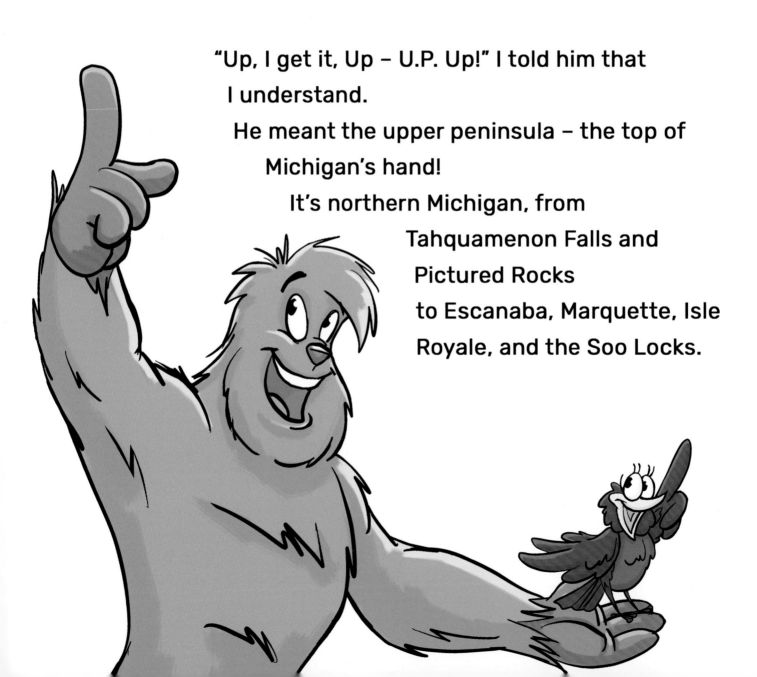

It's beautiful up there, and filled with Yoopers,
when he mentioned an island with pooper-scoopers.
Of course, Mackinac Island – it had to be,
just bikes, horses and carriages, really something to see!

I showed him the island and the Grand Hotel,
he was amazed by the longest porch,
he thought it was swell.
Named as one of the top 10 best places to stay,
the view of the Mackinac Bridge is incredible,
I must say.

Suddenly we heard a tune, and I knew the sound. . .
Why of course, it's Motown, we were Detroit city bound!
Known for music and the automotive industry,
but now it's been named the Comeback City.

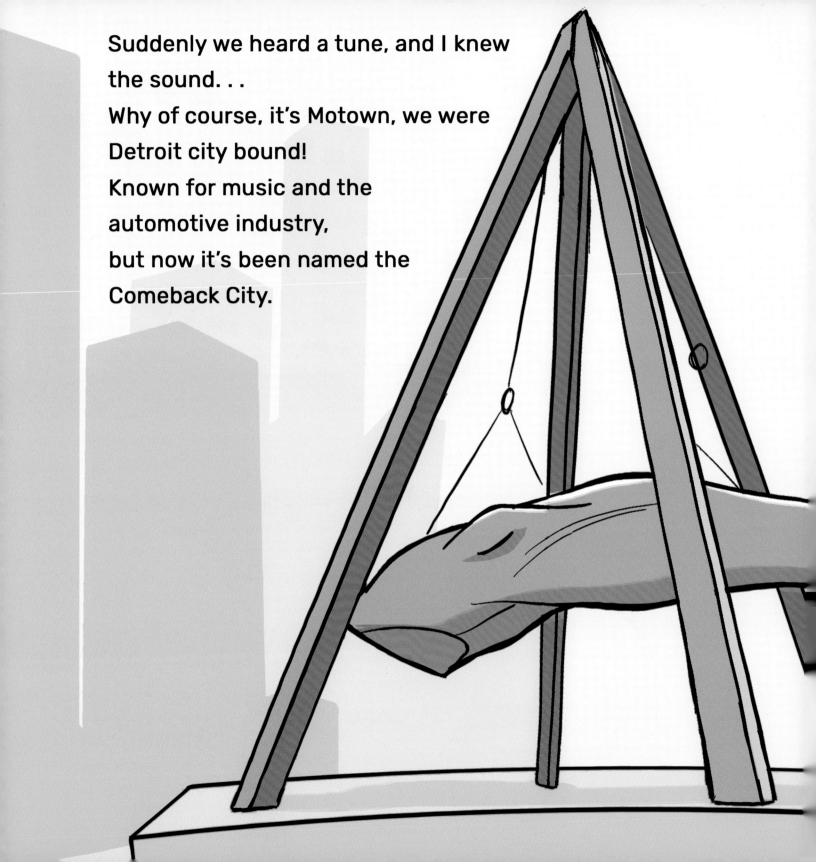

You know Detroit really deserves that title,
Michiganders are smart, resilient, and
re-made their city vital.

"Art," he said, and I had to agree.
We were at the Joe Louis Fist
 when it hit me.

"More art," he said. So, I was
thinking DIA,
The Detroit Institute of Arts –
one of the best in the USA.
Paintings, sculptures,
photographs, and more,
I could hardly wait, what a
great place to explore!

I asked him if his mitten looked like a painting.
He studied it when I said, "Hurry up, Big Guy. I'm waiting."
"Bigfoot," he insisted while shaking his head, 'no,'
and off to the next incredible painting we did go.

There were still so many places that we hadn't sleuthed,

ANN ARBOR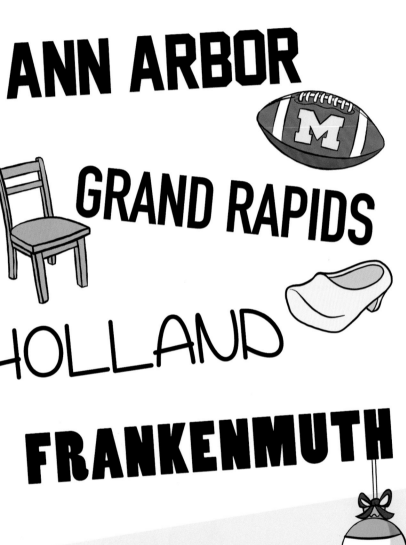

GRAND RAPIDS

HOLLAND

FRANKENMUTH

So much about Michigan is so pure,
but I started to think he was unsure.

I told him I thought he made up this whole mitten story.
"Like and inventor!" he smiled, and I was in my glory.
A lightbulb went off, and I knew just the place.
We were both so excited – we quickened our pace. . .

To the Greenfield Village for tours and fun,
attractions with interaction, history, and then some.
We headed to the Village and I was filled with glee,
as we drove around in a real Ford Model T.

Then to the Henry Ford Museum of American Innovation,
to explore the greatest inventions of our entire nation.
This museum is really very inspirational,
planes, trains and
automobiles, it's
just sensational.

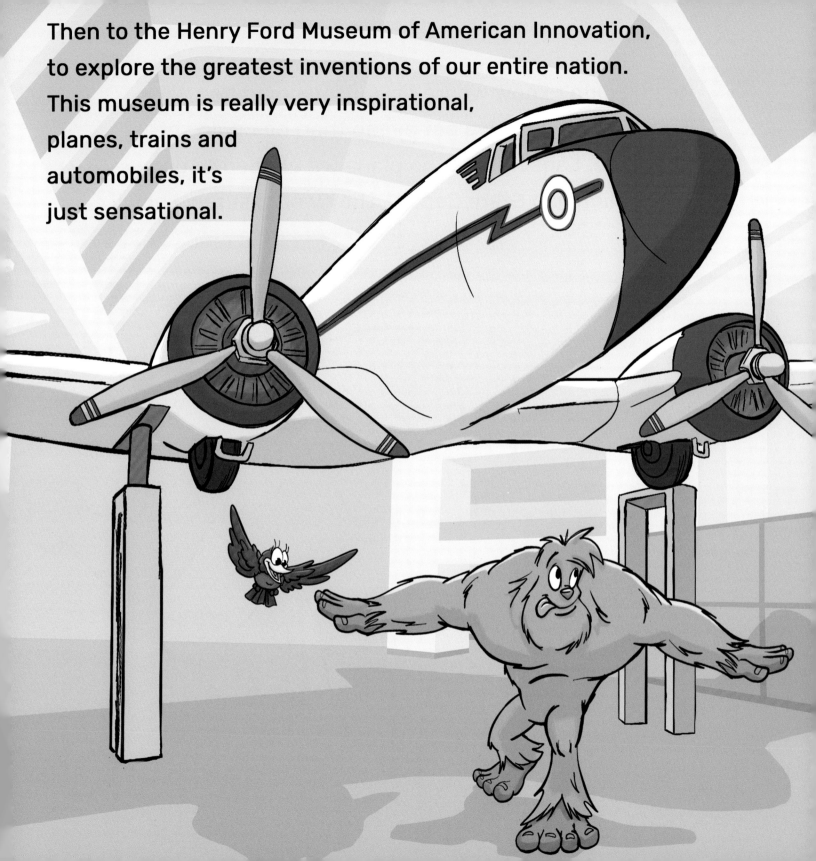

He still didn't know where his mitten could be.
I thought maybe if we got a map then he could see.
Of course, Lansing was the place we needed to go,
at the Michigan State Capitol, they would surely know!

It's where they take care of
everything in this state.
They are who we depend on to keep
Michigan great.
Michigan's government, legislature,
and state police too,
where they approve the Michigan
laws that get put through.

"Excuse me, have you seen my mitten?" Bigfoot politely inquired. I'm thinking *thank goodness, this Robin is tired.*

A lady smiled and said, "I always knew there was a Michigan Bigfoot. I'm pretty sure I can help you, now you two just stay put."

She pulled down a giant map of Michigan for us to see.

I was shocked, astounded, when it dawned on me.

I'm telling you, I really couldn't believe my eyes,

when she said his mitten is Michigan -

it was a huge surprise!

I should have known that, I'm Robin the state bird.

For goodness sake, why hadn't I heard?

I told him, "You didn't lose your mitten at all."

When he said, "Michigan is my mitten, now I recall!"

Yep, the mitten he thought he lost is really his home.

It's all the amazing places in this state that we roam.

From the U.P. to north, south,

and east to west,

it's the shape of your hand, it's

the place where we nest.

So, my friends, that's the story about whether Bigfoot is real,
and the wonderful Michigan mitten with all its appeal.
Now, I'm off because there's so much more to see. . .

"Hey, Big Guy would you just wait for me?"

MICHIGAN

State Capitol: Lansing

State Bird: Robin

State Fish: Brook Trout

State Reptile: Painted Turtle

State Game Mammal: White-Tailed Deer

State Flower: Apple Blossom

State Wildflower: Dwarf Lake Iris

State Rock: Petoskey Stone

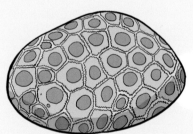

State Fossil: Mastodon

State Gem: Isle Royale Greenstone

State Tree: White Pine

State Soil: Kalkaska Sand

State Motto: "If you seek a pleasant peninsula, look about you."

Michigan is surrounded by four of the five Great Lakes - Erie, Huron, Michigan and Superior. The fifth Great Lake that does not border Michigan is Lake Ontario.

Michigan has 3,288 miles of shoreline, and is the longest freshwater coastline in the United States.

Bridges: The Mackinac Bridge connects Michigan's upper and lower peninsula.
The Sault Saint Marie International Bridge connects the twin cities of Sault Saint Marie, Michigan and Sault Saint Marie, Ontario, Canada.
The Blue Water Bridge connects Port Huron, Michigan and Sarnia, Ontario, Canada.
The Ambassador Bridge connects Detroit, Michigan and Windsor, Ontario, Canada.

Michigan lighthouses reach from one side of Michigan's shoreline to the other. There were once 247 lighthouses in Michigan that served the Great Lakes, and many are still in existence.

Nickname for Upper Peninsula people:
Yoopers
Nickname for Michigan people:
Michiganders

Michigan professional sports teams: Lions, Tigers, Red Wings, Pistons.

There's so much more to see in Michigan - wonderful zoo's, museum's, historical sites, parks, lakeshores, and waterfalls. The list of places goes on and on and on. So, now it's your turn to go explore this amazing state!

Karen Bell-Brege & Darrin Brege

This author-Illustrator, husband-wife team love monsters. They also love Michigan, writing and illustrating books for kids, and making people laugh. With an improv comedy and voice-over background they continue to present at hundreds of schools, events and associations every year.

Karen also teaches improv, and Darrin creates art and illustrations for top global brands along with mash-up posters. They happily reside in the mitten, and adore their very creative son, Mick. You can visit, and see all of their other books at **KarenandDarrin.com**

#1, All Isn't Well in ROSWELL!
written by K.B. Brege illustrated by D. Brege

#2, BIGFOOT...BIG TROUBLE!
written by K.B. Brege illustrated by D. Brege

#3, CHAMP...A Wave of Terror!
written by K.B. Brege illustrated by D. Brege

#4, Grudge of the GREMLINS!
written by K.B. Brege illustrated by D. Brege

#5, Abominable Snowman... A Frozen Nightmare
written by K.B. Brege illustrated by D. Brege

#6, Threatening Thunderbirds!
written by K.B. Brege illustrated by D. Brege

#1 London Screaming

#2 Aloha Haunts

#3 Ice Cavern Cadavers